Dedicated in loving memory of
Robert Natkin

Robert Natkin was a well known artist whose beautiful abstract paintings are comprised of many "little dabs of paint" which take on unique colors and elaborate shapes. His work has been exhibited in major museums and collections around the world.

Julian Frazin, a retired judge, has written many humorous plays and song lyrics for children and adults. He and his wife Rhona split their time between Chicago and Southwest Michigan, with their dog Cuddles, who was the inspiration for his first childrens' book "Cuddles the Cattle Dog—a new Christmas tail."

Susan Schirmer is a Michigan native. Her art background includes both fine and graphic arts. She works out of her studio at the Box Factory for the Arts in St. Joseph, Michigan. This is her third children's book project. She also illustrated "Cuddles the Cattle Dog" for author, Julian Frazin and recently "How Noel Saved Christmas" by Christine Knuth.

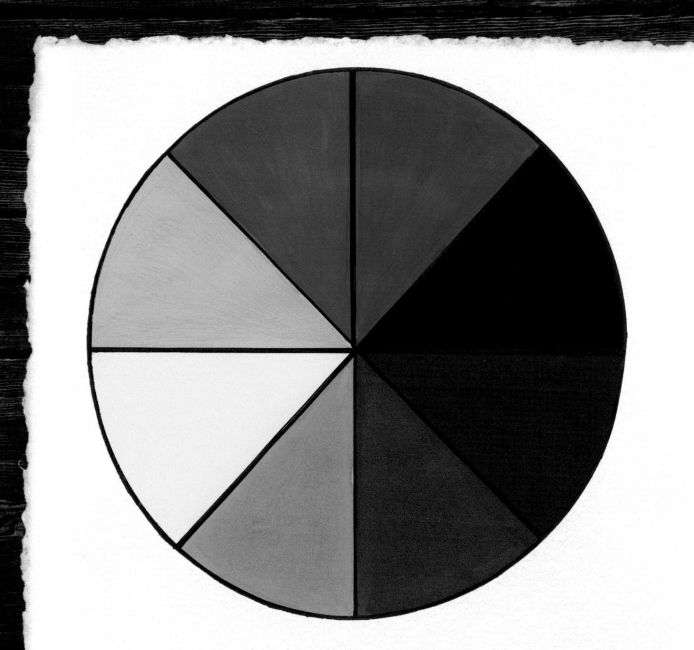

Berwick Court Publishing
Chicago, IL

Written by Julian Frazin
Illustrations by Susan Schirmer
Music by Larry Novak
Layout by Danielle Hill – Trungale Egan

ISBN: 978-0-9838846-5-1

Printed in the USA

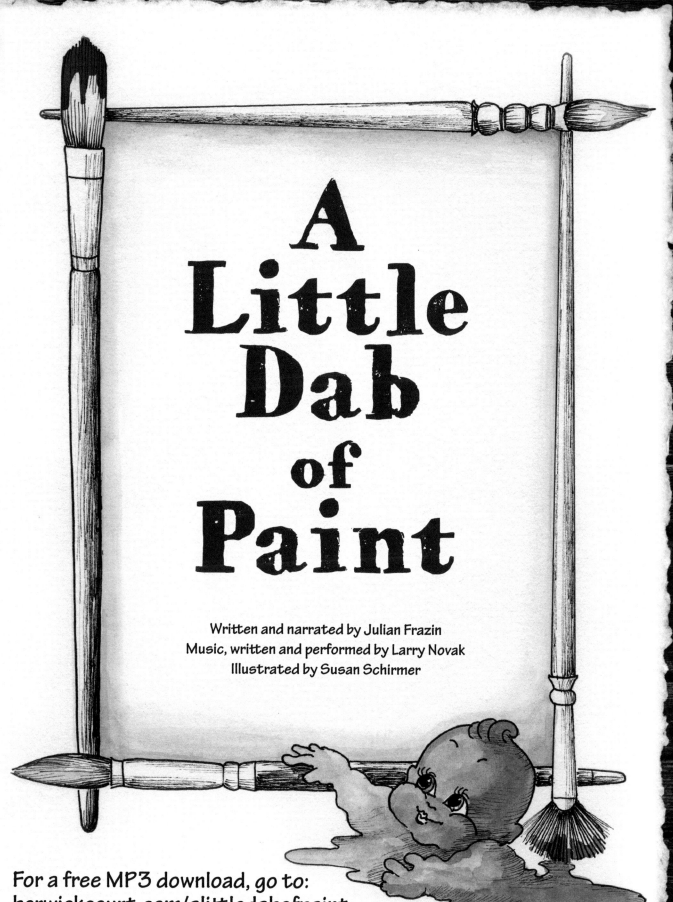

A Little Dab of Paint

Written and narrated by Julian Frazin
Music, written and performed by Larry Novak
Illustrated by Susan Schirmer

For a free MP3 download, go to:
berwickcourt.com/alittledabofpaint

This is a tale short and quaint,
About a little dab of paint,
That accidentally dripped down on the floor.

Now how it happened, who could say,
Perhaps the artist looked away,
I'm sure that happened
many times before.

For on that floor
　　were lots of spots,
Of every shade and hue,
　　Each color has
　　　　a different name,
And ours was "Baby Blue."

Now that's when a
Yellow came along,
And began to
sing this little song,
Saying, " Blue and Yellow
can make Green."

"Oh, Yellow and Blue make Green,
Yellow and Blue make Green,
It's the finest color I've ever seen,
On grass or a lime or a lima bean,
Grass or a lime or a lima bean,
Yellow and Blue make Green."

And then another color said,
"Hey there Blue, my name is Red,
As for me, a Green could not be duller,
But if you will become my friend,

I'm sure we'll make the perfect blend,
Purple - to make a horse of a different color."

"Oh, **Purple** comes from **Red** and **Blue**,

Purple comes from **Red** and **Blue**,

And I think it's time you knew,

On a plum, a grape or a lollipop, too,

A plum, a grape or a lollipop, too,

Purple comes from

Red and **Blue**."

Then Yellow turned to **Red** and said,

"I've got a great idea, instead,

Of being Green or **Purple**, let's agree,

Another color we could find,

Now Orange is one that comes to mind,

And all we really need is you and me."

"Oh, **Red** and Yellow make Orange,
Red and Yellow make Orange,
On a tangerine and, of course, an orange,
A tangerine and, of course, an orange,
There are no words that
rhyme with Orange,
"**Red** and Yellow make Orange,"

Baby Blue began to frown,

"This conversation gets me down,

For to my family colors I must be true."

"My mom is Alice Blue, you see,

My father's Navy Blue, and me,

I hope to someday to be a Royal Blue."

That is when the Yellow said,

"Before I get too old,

I hope one day that I will be,

a shining Solid Gold."

Red said, "There's much one can be,
And if it were up to me,
I would be a **Fire Engine Red**."

The three decided then and there,
  They would have to go elsewhere,
To become the colors they were hoping for.

But when they tried to leave that spot,
  They quickly learned that they could not.
For they dried up and were stuck to the floor.

As there they lay, from year to year,
Other colors would appear.
Turquoise, **Salmon**, Jade and Puce,
Magenta and Chatreuse.
Every hue and every shade,
But one day, in came a maid.

Who decided it was time

TO CLEAN THE FLOOR!

And all the colors sang:

Please! Don't clean the floor!

Oh please! Don't clean the floor!

    For if you should wash down that floor,

Us colors here will be no more,

And, as we said two times before,

PLEASE DON'T CLEAN THE FLOOR!

Before the Artist could say, "Stop,"
The maid had taken out her mop,
And quickly started scrubbing down the floor.

All the paints began to run,
Each into another one,
Until the separate colors were no more.

The Artist cried, "I said to cease,
Those colors now have blurred."
The maid said, "Open up your eyes,
A MIRACLE HAS OCCURRED!"

And as the tale has been told,
There was a streak of *Solid Gold*,
Of **Fire Engine Red** and **Royal Blue**!

The artist looked and got inspired,

For those were colors she admired,

She figured out a way to use them all.

And now those friends will never part,

They're all in a work of art,

A masterpiece that's hanging on the wall...

Each color in this little tale,

Has sung a special song,

Just like you learned your ABC's,

NOW YOU CAN SING ALONG!

"Oh, Yellow and Blue make Green,

Yellow and Blue make Green,

It's the finest colors I've ever seen,

On grass or a lime or a lima bean,

Grass or a lime or a lima bean,

Yellow and Blue make Green."

"Oh, **Purple** comes from **Red** and **Blue**,
 Purple comes from **Red** and **Blue**,
And I think it's time you knew,
 On a plum, a grape or a lollipop, too,
A plum, a grape or a lollipop, too,
 Purple comes from **Red** and **Blue**."

"**Red** and **Yellow** make **Orange**,
Red and **Yellow** make **Orange**,
On a tangerine and, of course, an orange,
A tangerine and,
of course, an orange,
There are no words
that rhyme with **Orange**,"
"**Red** and **Yellow** make **Orange**,

Red and Yellow and Blue,
Red and Yellow and Blue,
Every color must come through,
Every tint and shade and hue,
Add some White
and a little **Black** too,
Red and Yellow and Blue.
RED...AND YELLOW...AND BLUE!

THE END

CPSIA information can be obtained
at www.ICGtesting.com
Printed in the USA
LVIC04n1615190713
343751LV00001B